For Oscar!

Published by Sourcebooks Jabberwocky, an imprint of Sourcebooks, Inc.
P.O. Box 4410, Naperville, Illinois 60567-4410
(630) 961-3900
Fax: (630) 961-2168
www.sourcebooks.com

First published by Scholastic Press, a division of Scholastic Australia Pty Limited, in 2015.
This edition is published under license from Scholastic Australia Pty Limited.

Library of Congress Cataloging-in-Publication data is on file with the publisher.

Source of Production: Leo Paper, Heshan City, Guangdong Province, China
Date of Production: March 2016
Run Number: 5005636
Printed and bound in China.
LEO 10 9 8 7 6 5 4 3 2 1

More than anything else in the whole wide world, I wanna be a

great
BIG
DINOSAUR!

Excuse me.

Did I hear correctly? Do you want, more than **anything** else in the whole wide world, to be a **GREAT big DINOSAUR?**

GASP!

YES, I do!

Wonderful!

Well, I know **ALL** there is to know about being a **GREAT big DINOSAUR!**

And first, you must learn how to . . .

PING!

I love STOMPING!

What else do we do?

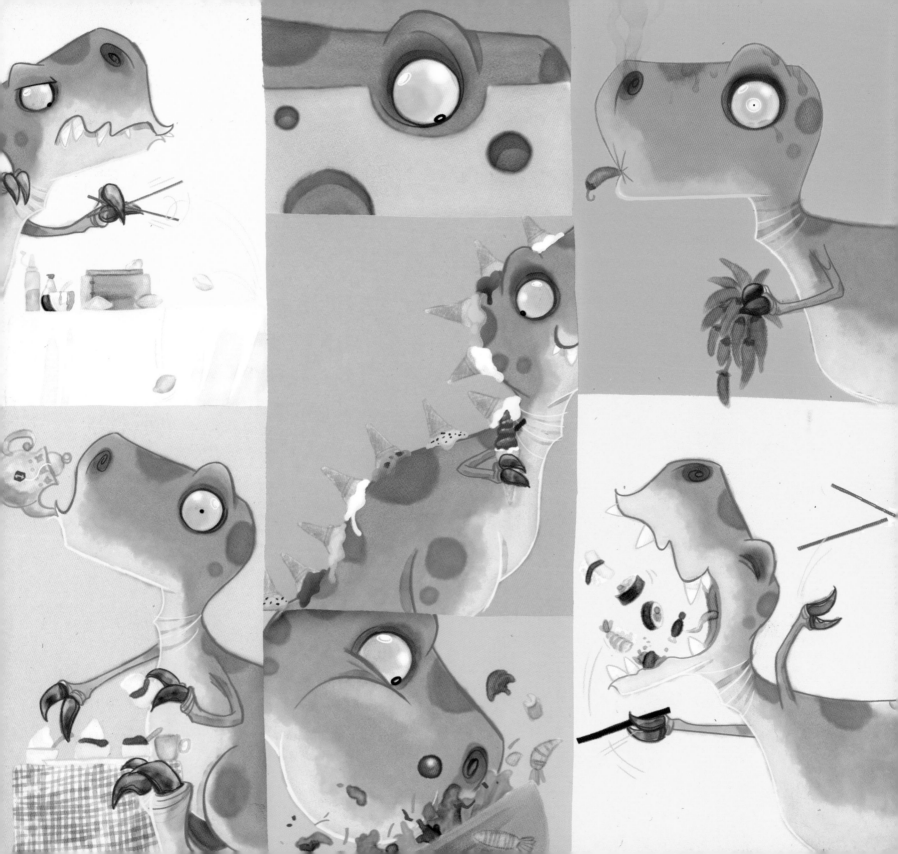

I also like reading!

Do **DINOSAURS** read?

Not often, **no.**

What about soccer?

Do DINOSAURS
play soccer?

**Not really,
no.**
I'm not very good with my arms . . .

OOH!

PERFECT!
You use your feet!

I don't suppose dinosaurs
play video games either.

Well, it's nearly time for dinner! I'd better go! Thanks for showing me how to be a

great

B
DINO

Hmm.

Maybe . . .

more than
anything
else in the
whole wide world . . .

Let's be
BOTH!